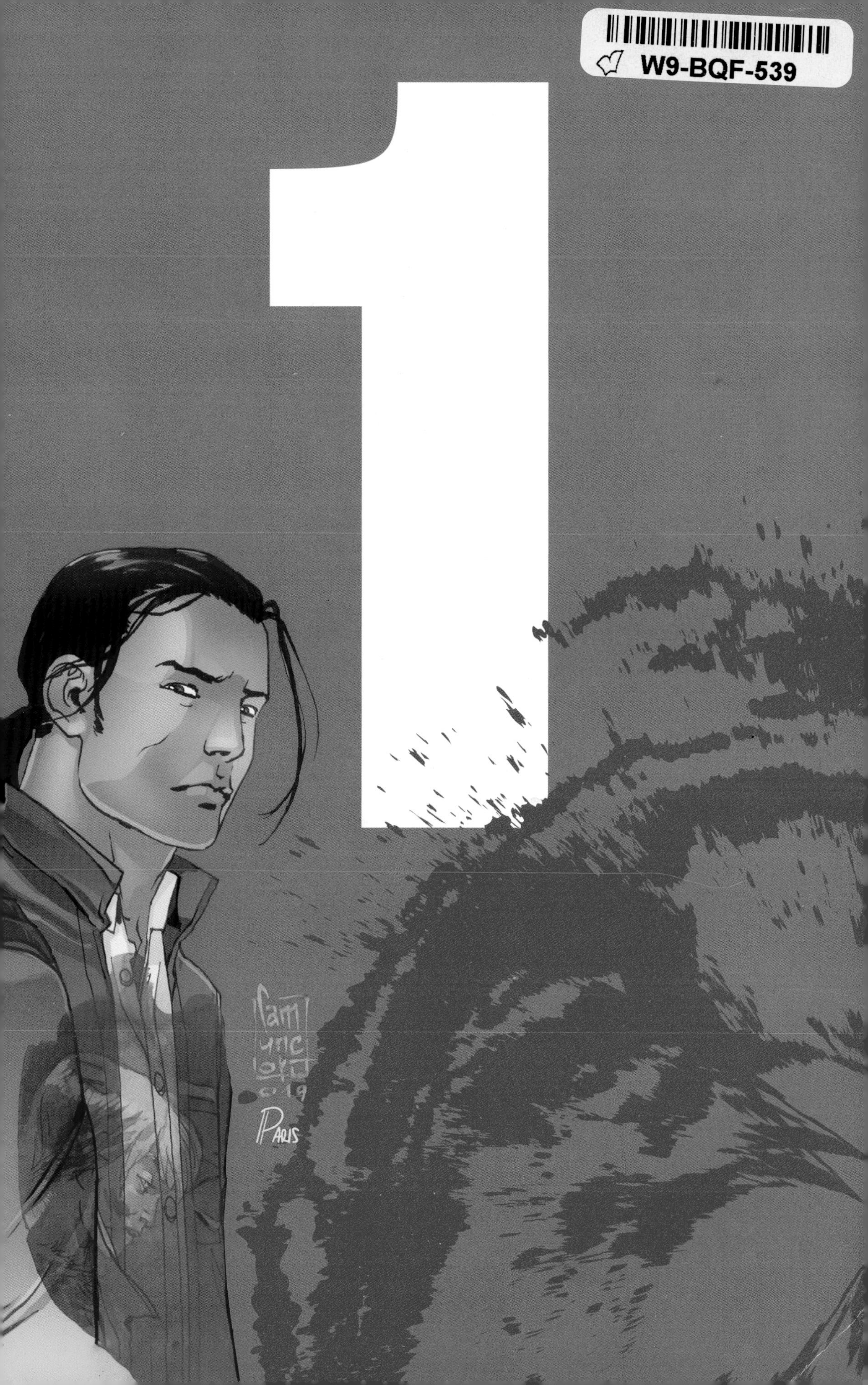
1

OUR WORLD'S DNA IS CHANGING.

UNPRECEDENTED TECTONIC SHIFTS.
SPONTANEOUS, RADICAL CHANGES IN THE ECO SYSTEMS.

IN MOMENTS OF UNIMAGINABLE AGITATION,
THE HUMAN RACE ACTS OUT IN UNIMAGINABLE WAYS.

AND THOSE ARE JUST INDIVIDUAL SPECIES. NOW EARTH ITSELF IS PUSHING BACK.

CERTAIN PEOPLE WORLDWIDE ARE ... CHANGING. *TRANSFORMING*.

IGNITING WITH *POWER*.

H1 IGNITION

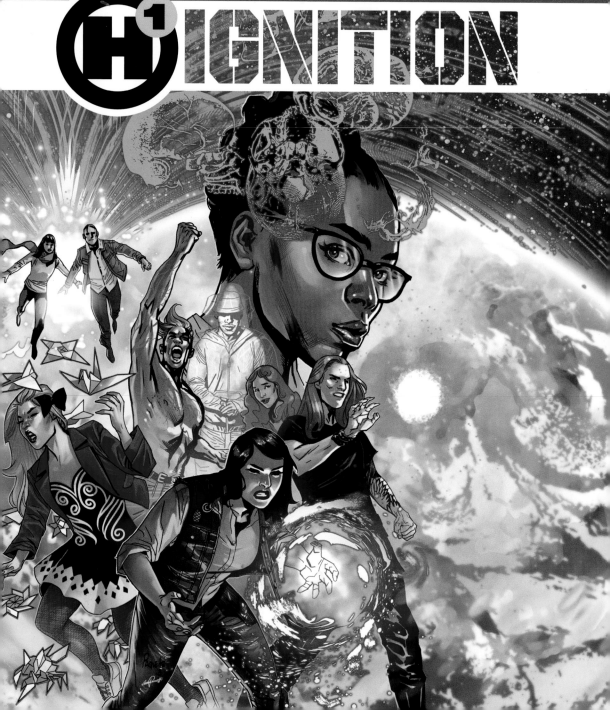

MAGS VISAGGIO | DARCIE LITTLE BADGER | GUILLERMO SANNA

STRANGELANDS

VOLUME ONE | LOVE + CHAOS

IGNITION

STRANGELANDS

WRITERS | **MAGS VISAGGIO** AND
DARCIE LITTLE BADGER
ARTIST | **GUILLERMO SANNA**
COLOR ARTIST | **BRYAN VALENZA**
COVER | **DAN PANOSIAN**

TITLE PAGE IILUSTRATION | **MIKE MCKONE** AND
LEONARDO PACIAROTTI
BACK COVER AND PAGES 2–3 IILUSTRATION | **GIUSEPPE CAMUNCOLI**
AND **PARIS ALLEYNE**
PAGE 4 ILLUSTRATION | **YANICK PAQUETTE** AND
LEONARDO PACIAROTTI
LETTERS | **A LARGER WORLD STUDIOS**

SHARED UNIVERSE BASED ON CONCEPTS CREATED WITH
KWANZA OSAJYEFO, CARLA SPEED MCNEIL, YANICK PAQUETTE

DIRECTOR OF CREATIVE DEVELOPMENT | **MARK WAID**
CHIEF CREATIVE OFFICER | **JOHN CASSADAY**
SENIOR EDITOR | **FABRICE SAPOLSKY**
ASSISTANT EDITOR | **AMANDA LUCIDO**
LOGO DESIGN | **RIAN HUGHES**
SENIOR ART DIRECTOR | **JERRY FRISSEN**

CEO AND PUBLISHER | **FABRICE GIGER**
COO | **ALEX DONOGHUE**
CFO | **GUILLAUME NOUGARET**
DIRECTOR OF SALES AND MARKETING | **AILEN LUJO**
SALES AND MARKETING ASSISTANT | **ANDREA TORRES**
SALES REPRESENTATIVE | **HARLEY SALBACKA**
PRODUCTION COORDINATOR | **ALISA TRAGER**
DIRECTOR, LICENSING | **EDMOND LEE**
CTO | **BRUNO BARBERI**
RIGHTS AND LICENSING | **LICENSING@HUMANOIDS.COM**
PRESS AND SOCIAL MEDIA | **PR@HUMANOIDS.COM**

STRANGELANDS VOL 1: LOVE + CHAOS This title is a publication of Humanoids, Inc. 8033 Sunset
Blvd. #628, Los Angeles, CA 90046. Copyright © 2019 Humanoids, Inc., Los Angeles (USA). All
rights reserved. Humanoids and its logos are ® and © 2019 Humanoids, Inc.
Library of Congress Control Number: 2019910049

This volume collects STRANGELANDS issues 1–4.

H1 is an imprint of Humanoids, Inc.

HUMANOIDS

THE
UNITED
STATES
THE COLORADO MOUNTAINS

PEOPLE'S REPUBLIC OF
CHINA
SHANGHAI

VRRRRRRRRRRRRR

WHY CAN'T YOU USE A KNIFE?

ANYTHING BUT *THAT*... THAT THING. I'M AFRAID OF THEM.

DON'T BE.

ADAM! YOU'VE GOT TO GO FASTER!

I'M GOING AS FAST AS I CAN, ELAKSHI!

WE'LL GET TOO FAR APART!

BLAM BLAM BLAM

PLNG

PLNG

PLNG

THIS JELLYFISH IS GOING TO HEAL YOU.

ESPECIALLY BECAUSE OF YOUR THALASSOPHOBIA.

THIS AGAIN, DUDE?

GIMME.

AND THAT. WHAT'S NEXT?

TWO GUNS? WHERE DO YOU KEEP THEM ALL?

NNG!

IT'S OKAY, JASON. I PROMISE. LET IT STING.

ADAM! YOUR POWERS!

TRY PULLING THE TRAIN TOWARDS YOU.

MY ATTRACTION SKILLS AREN'T *THAT* STRONG!

I PROMISE.

VRRRMMMWOOOMF

GET BACK ON YOUR BIKE!

BEFORE IT'S TOO LATE!

OH GOD, IT'S STARTING.

OH, **GREAT.**

IF ALL HELL BREAKS LOOSE, IT'S **YOUR** FAULT, PAL.

COME ON COME ON COME ON.

IF EVER THERE WAS A TIME FOR THIS DAMNED **REPELLING FIELD** OF MINE TO NOT WORK, IT'S NOW.

SKREEE4N3KK

ELAKSHI!

STAY BACK!

NO? OKAY. WORTH A TRY.

SO IS THIS...

THNK

ALRIGHT, TRAIN, GET BACK HERE.

YOU'RE SIX THOUSAND TONS OF SCREAMING METAL AND I'M 180 POUNDS OF HUMAN MAGNET BUT--

WHAT THE--?!

TUCK YOUR CHIN WHEN YOU LAND!

KLANG

CATCH THIS!

THE NINJA CLAW. NEAT.

GLAD YOU STILL HAVE IT, THANKS!

WHAT THE HELL WAS *THAT,* ADAM?

"ME TRYING TO ESCAPE *THE TERMINATOR!*"

13

DIDN'T YOU SEE OUR FAVORITE HOMICIDAL STALKER *SHOOTING AT ME?* ON A *MOTORCYCLE?*

HE'S *ALWAYS* SHOOTING AT US. YOU SHOULD KNOW BY NOW TO STAY CALM AND KEEP CLOSE.

NOBODY ASKED FOR A LECTURE, ELAKSHI.

GOD SAVE ME, BUT THE WHIMS OF FATE HAVE BOUND US TOGETHER. THAT MAKES YOUR RASH DECISIONS MY BUSINESS.

YOU KNOW WHAT HAPPENS IF WE GET TOO FAR APART. AND YOU WERE WILLING TO RISK THAT.

I WAS. YOU WERE *THERE,* EL. HE SHOWED UP OUT OF NOWHERE LIKE HE *ALWAYS DOES.* I'M SORRY MY *RASH INSTINCT* WAS TO GET YOU ON THE TRAIN BEFORE HE KILLED YOU.

NEXT TIME, WE CAN DIE TOGETHER. SOUND BETTER?

YOU *KNOW* THAT'S NOT WHAT I WANT.

LOOK. I'M JUST FRUSTRATED. SHANGHAI WAS YET ANOTHER DEAD END IN THIS *INTERMINABLE* QUEST TO RID OURSELVES OF THESE AWFUL ABILITIES. THIS--

"...WAS THE WORST THING TO EVER HAPPEN TO US." I KNOW. YOU SAY IT.

A LOT.

JUST BECAUSE YOU FIND IT ANNOYING DOESN'T MEAN IT ISN'T TRUE.

14

IS IT *REALLY* TRUE, THOUGH?

LOOK, I DON'T LOVE THAT IF WE GET SEPARATED BY TOO MUCH DISTANCE THINGS START TO GO KABLOOEY, BUT--

HOLD THAT THOUGHT.

DEET DEET

Do you believe in magic?

38.198521, -103.751687

Air China Flight Z 1181 direct to Denver.

OUR MYSTERIOUS BENEFACTOR AT WORK.

THINK IT'S WORTH IT? THESE WATCHES ARE THE BEST THING SHE'S GIVEN US. AND THEY AREN'T *THAT* GREAT.

WELL, KITTYHAWK HASN'T FOUND US A CURE *YET*. BUT IT'S EITHER KEEP MOVING OR LET *MUSCLES* BACK THERE FINALLY KILL US.

Here is your flight confirmation.

DAMN. THE WOMAN WORKS FAST.

WELL, THEN.

"NEXT STOP, DENVER."

15

VASQUEZ COLORADO
TWO HOURS SOUTH OF DENVER

THIS PLACE LOOKS LIKE A SKI RESORT.

YOU THINK THESE PEOPLE ARE ON THE LEVEL?

KITTYHAWK SENT US HERE FOR A REASON.

THEN AGAIN, MAYBE SHE JUST THOUGHT WE NEEDED SOME R&R. AFTER THE LAST FEW CITIES. I MEAN, SHANGHAI, BANGKOK, WELLINGTON...

DON'T EVEN TALK ABOUT WELLINGTON. I'LL BE HAVING NIGHTMARES ABOUT GIANT CRICKETS TILL I DIE.

DO YOU SEE THAT SIGN? HOW CAN I BE HOME AND ON A JOURNEY AT THE SAME TIME?

WILD SAINTS: WELCOME HOME. YOUR JOURNEY IS JUST BEGINNING

MAYBE THEY KNOW MY AUNTIE. SHE LIVED IN AN RV.

I DOUBT DRIVING 'ROUND TEXAS IS MUCH OF A JOURNEY, THOUGH.

HEY, THERE! I'M ELISE, AND I'D LIKE TO OFFICIALLY WELCOME YOU TO WILD SAINTS! WILL YOU BE CHECKING IN?

A FRIEND OF OURS RECOMMENDED WE TAKE A LOOK. SAID YOU'RE ABLE TO...DEAL WITH PROBLEMS LIKE OURS.

OH, ABSOLUTELY!

LET ME SHOW YOU AROUND, AND WE CAN TALK ABOUT WHAT WILD SAINTS CAN DO FOR YOU!

Wild Saints

16

WILD SAINTS WAS FOUNDED EIGHT MONTHS AGO BY DR. WINSOME FLETCHER, A PSYCHOLOGICAL RESEARCHER FROM MELBOURNE, WITH ONE MISSION...

...TO USE PEOPLE LIKE YOU TO ELEVATE *ALL OF HUMANITY.*

"WINSOME"?

ALL LIFE *NATURALLY* GENERATES VITAL ENERGY. THIS *COLLECTIVE CONSCIOUSNESS ENERGY,* OR CCE, CRADLES MOTHER EARTH LIKE THE MAGNETIC FIELD.

AND I *KNOW* IT'S NOT YOUR INTENTION, BUT...

...BY HOARDING CCE, WHICH FUELS YOUR ABNORMAL ABILITIES, YOU'RE *HURTING* OUR PLANET.

THE EFFECTS OF THAT HAVE BEEN... STRANGE. NEW, OFTEN UNWELCOME ABILITIES SEEM TO BE CROPPING UP AT ALARMING RATES.

MANY OF THE PEOPLE LIVING AT WILD SAINTS ARE LIKE *YOU.* RECIPIENTS OF *TERRIBLE* POWER.

ALTHOUGH HIS DISCOVERIES ARE NOT ACCEPTED BY THE NARROW-MINDED GATEKEEPERS OF SCIENCE...

...DR. FLETCHER FOUND THAT THE RAPID CORRUPTION OF HUMANITY HAS CAUSED CCE TO POOL IN *POCKETS* AROUND INDIVIDUALS, RATHER THAN TO DISTRIBUTE EVENLY.

AND I'M SURE I DON'T HAVE TO TELL YOU THE CONSEQUENCES OF THAT. NATURAL DISASTERS AND HUMAN TRAGEDY CONSISTENTLY FOLLOW THESE ERUPTIONS OF POWER.

SO, WHAT HAPPENS *HERE?*

DR. FLETCHER HYPOTHESIZES THAT, THROUGH PHYSICAL DISCIPLINE UNDER CAREFUL MEDICAL SUPERVISION, THIS ENERGY CAN BE DISPERSED.

REMOVING ANY ACCOMPANYING POWERS IN THE PROCESS?

EXACTLY! AND RETURNING THAT ENERGY TO THE GLOBAL POOL OF CCE TO BENEFIT ALL OF HUMANITY!

DOES IT WORK?

NOT *ONLY* DOES IT WORK...

17

...BUT IT DOESN'T REQUIRE A DAY-ONE PATCH, EITHER.

OH! THIS WOULD BE DR. FLETCHER HIMSELF!

PLEASE, CALL ME WIN.

I'M ASSUMING YOU TWO ARE THE LANDS? MARRIED LONG?

MARRIED? NO. WE GET THAT A LOT, THOUGH. MAYBE IT'S A SIGN.

STOP JOKING. ADAM AND I JUST HAVE THE SAME LAST NAME. IT'S ENTIRELY COINCIDENTAL.

OR FATE.

PLEASE BEHAVE.

HOW DID YOU KNOW OUR NAMES, ANYWAY?

YOUR, AHEM, BENEFACTOR CALLED AHEAD. ALL THE ARRANGEMENTS HAVE BEEN MADE, IF YOU WANT TO PARTICIPATE IN OUR PROGRAM. DO YOU KNOW HOW LUCKY YOU ARE TO HAVE HER?

DOESN'T ALWAYS FEEL LIKE IT.

DEEP POCKETS, THAT ONE.

I'LL TAKE IT FROM HERE, ELISE. DO YOU HAVE ANY QUESTIONS ABOUT WILD SAINTS OR OUR PROCESS?

I'M CURIOUS ABOUT THE INTERIOR DESIGN. WHERE'D YOU GET THAT MEDICINE WHEEL? A GAS STATION?

I TAKE NATIVE SPIRITUALITY VERY SERIOUSLY.

DO YOU?

18

HOW DO YOU...*DISPERSE* CCE? WE'VE BEEN ALL OVER THE *WORLD* TRYING TO FIND A SOLUTION TO OUR PROBLEM.

A VARIETY OF WAYS. WE START WITH MEDITATION AND CENTERING. MOST OF THE TIME THAT SEEMS TO BE ENOUGH. BUT, FOR SOME STUBBORN CASES...

...IT TAKES SOMETHING MORE... INTENSE.

INTENSE LIKE *HOW?*

DAMN! WILL YOU TAKE A LOOK AT THAT, MATE? COLORADO IS GOD'S OWN COUNTRY. I'M CONVINCED OF IT.

HOW HARD IS YOUR SITUATION? BEING STUCK TOGETHER LIKE THIS ALL THE TIME? AND FOR ALMOST A *YEAR.*

CAN'T HAVE BEEN EASY.

SO KITTYHAWK TOLD YOU ABOUT US?

NO, IT HASN'T BEEN EASY. IF WE GET TOO FAR APART? OR IF WE GET TOO CLOSE AND TOUCH?

CHAOS.

TELL YOU WHAT. YOU'RE ALREADY PAID UP. WHY DON'T THE TWO OF YOU RELAX AND ENJOY YOUR STAY?

THERE'S A SESSION TONIGHT AT EIGHT IF YOU WANT TO COME AND SEE WHAT WE DO. NO PRESSURE...

19

"...BUT I THINK YOU'LL LIKE WHAT YOU SEE."

I DON'T LIKE THIS.

YOU *NEVER* DO. WHAT IS IT THIS TIME?

DID YOU NOTICE HOW HE DODGED MY QUESTION?

ADAM--

I ASKED HIM *POINT BLANK* WHAT HE MEANT BY "MORE INTENSE," AND HE JUST STARTED TALKING ABOUT HOW MUCH HE LOVED COLORADO!

AND ALL THIS INDIAN KITSCH BRINGS BACK TERRIBLE MEMORIES OF PAPER TEEPEES AND CHICKEN FEATHER HEAD-DRESSES. TRUST ME. YOU DO *NOT* WANT TO BE THE ONLY APACHE KID AT SUMMER CAMP.

HONESTLY, THIS ALL REEKS TO ME.

LISTEN, THE ONLY REASON WE'RE HERE IS TO HAVE THESE STUPID POWERS TAKEN AWAY. WIN MAY BE NINETY PERCENT NONSENSE, BUT IF THE REMAINING TEN PERCENT CAN HELP US, I HONESTLY *DON'T CARE* HOW HE DOES THE JOB.

WE'RE TICKING TIME BOMBS, ADAM. AND MY ABILITY TO *REPEL OBJECTS* IS *ONE HUNDRED* PERCENT NOT WORTH THE COST.

OR HAVE YOU FORGOTTEN WHAT HAPPENED LAST TIME WE WENT KABLOOEY?

WE DON'T EVEN KNOW IF HE'S EVEN *TALKING* ABOUT PEOPLE LIKE US. MIGHT JUST BE A SCAM ARTIST TRYING TO SEPARATE GULLIBLE KITTYHAWKS FROM THEIR MONEY.

YOU CAN ATTEND THIS "SESSION" IF YOU WANT. *I'M* GOING TO TAKE A WALK.

DON'T STRAY TOO FAR AND--

--DON'T FORGET TO CHECK MY WATCH. RIGHT-O.

20

23
METRES

Wild
ints

PLK

PLK

PLK

PLK

21

GOD *DAMMIT,* ADAM.

105 METRES

THERE'S A DIRTY LITTLE SECRET THAT NOBODY WANTS YOU TO KNOW. BUT IT'S THE KEY TO THE WHOLE UNIVERSE.

THIS ENERGY ISN'T JUST FOR YOU. IT'S FOR *EVERYBODY.*

I THINK THERE'S A LEVEL WHERE WE KNOW THAT.

HOW MANY PEOPLE LIKE US HAVE GIVEN OF THEMSELVES OVER THE YEARS FOR THE BETTERMENT OF MAN? HOW MANY *SAINTS* AND *SAGES?*

BUT HOW MANY *TYRANTS* AND *MURDERERS* HAS IT GIVEN US, TOO? IT'S A PROBLEM OF *SCARCITY.*

"OUR POPULATION HAS GROWN SO MUCH SO FAST THAT COLLECTIVE CONSCIOUSNESS ENERGY IS *POOLING* INSTEAD OF REACHING EVERYONE.

"SO IT'S UP TO US TO TAKE OUR OWN CCE...

"...AND MAKE IT A GIFT."

WHUMP WHUMP WHUMP

WHUMP

WHUMP

WHUMP

22

HEY!

WHUMF

WHAT ARE YOU DOING? ARE YOU ALL RIGHT?

DO YOU NEED HELP?

I AM HELPING.

ALL THE HURT, ALL THE PAIN, ALL THE DAMNED PHYSICAL AND EMOTIONAL TRAUMA THAT ACCOMPANIED OUR IGNITIONS. WE GIVE IT UP.

THAT'S HOW WE SAVE THE WORLD.

23

I WANT YOU TO **JOIN** ME, TO HELP TAKE ALL OF **OUR** PAIN AND **OUR** HARDSHIP AND TRANSMUTE IT. TRANSFORM IT.

AND IN TRANSFORMING OURSELVES--

CLAP CLAP CLAP CLAP CLAP CLAP

--TRANSFORM ALL HUMANITY.

CLAP CLAP CLAP CLAP CLAP CLAP CLAP CLAP CLAP

24

I JUST WANT IT TO GO AWAY. I'VE HURT SO MANY PEOPLE.

I JUST WANT TO HELP SAVE THE WORLD.

I KNOW.

BELIEVE ME, I KNOW.

IDEN   AUTO

UTC - 22:38

DMS
34°28'47.59" N
118°18'59.65" W

UTC

YEAH, I FOUND THIS SPOT YESTERDAY. *REALLY* AMAZING VIEW OF THE LAKE.

YOU'LL JUST--

--LOVE IT.

HM.

EXCUSE ME, SIR, THIS IS PRIVATE--

SHNNK

SLIT

TING. TING.

HNNG.

UNNG... NOT RIGHT NOW.

YES SIR.

THE LANDS WILL BE DEAD WITHIN THE WEEK.

EVEN IF IT KILLS ME.

2

DID YOU SLEEP AT *ALL* LAST NIGHT?

VASQUEZ COLORADO
TWO HOURS SOUTH OF DENVER

HOW *COULD* I?

THE WOMAN I FOUND WASN'T JUST INJURED. SHE HAD MULTIPLE METACARPAL FRACTURES AND FULL THICKNESS DEGLOVING INJURIES OVER ALL FOUR METACARPOPHALANGEAL JOINTS.

ONCE AGAIN FOR PEOPLE WHO DIDN'T DROP OUT OF MED SCHOOL?

SHE'D PUNCHED HER HANDS TO PIECES.

THE POOR THING NEEDS TO BE IN A HOSPITAL. A *REAL* HOSPITAL. BUT THEY TOOK HER WHEN WE RETURNED TO THE LODGE.

WHO TOOK HER?

WILD SAINTS COUNSELORS.

THEY CHUCKED HER ON A STRETCHER AND--

CHANGE INTO THIS.

--CARRIED HER INTO A CREEPY BUILDING DOWN THE HILL.

YOU MEAN THE ON-SITE CLINIC?

YES. THE ONE WITH ARMED GUARDS.

AND BARS ON THE WINDOWS.

WHY DOES A LODGE NEED A WHOLE CLINIC, ANYWAY?

29

PROBABLY BECAUSE WE'RE AN HOUR AWAY FROM THE NEAREST HOSPITAL.

I'M *STILL* GOING TO INVESTIGATE.

LIKE. EVERY. TIME.

LOOK. I'M SORRY YOU HAD SUCH A BAD EXPERIENCE. *TRULY!* BUT THAT WOMAN WAS CLEARLY TROUBLED.

YEAH. YEAH, SHE WAS.

I HAVE A SESSION WITH WIN IN FIVE MINUTES.

WE CAN DISCUSS THIS LATER.

Wild Saints

ALL MEALS WILL BE SERVED IN THE DINING ROOM ONLY

AFTERNOON TEA WILL BE SERVED IN THE SITTING ROOM

MEAL TIMINGS ARE:

BREAKFAST
LUNCH
AFTERNOON TEA

GET SOME SLEEP.

BE CAREFUL, EL.

"I DON'T TRUST HIM."

ELAKSHI, FOR THIS PROCESS TO WORK, I NEED SOMETHING FROM YOU.

COMMITMENT.

30

WILL YOU GIVE THAT TO ME?

OF COURSE. I NEVER DO ANYTHING HALF-ARSED.

I SUSPECTED AS MUCH. YOUR FRIEND *ADAM* DOESN'T SHARE YOUR DRIVE.

"WELL. HE DIDN'T HAVE MY PARENTS GROWING UP."

"WERE THEY STRICT?"

"DEMANDING. WHEN I TOLD THEM THAT I WANTED TO BE A DANCER...

"...THEY SENT ME TO THE BEST INSTRUCTORS.

"ATTENDED ALL MY RECITALS.

"ENCOURAGED ME TO BE THE *BEST.*

"MUM AND DAD SHOWED ME WHAT IT TAKES TO BE COMMITTED.

"EVERYTHING."

"AT FIRST, I RESENTED THEM. WHAT WAS THE POINT?

"TO MOST OF THE WORLD, MY **COMMITMENT** DIDN'T MATTER.

"THE HARDER I WORKED?

CLUNK

"THE BETTER I GOT?

"THE MORE **SOME** PEOPLE HATED ME."

"OVER TIME, I LEARNED THE IMPORTANCE OF BEING THE BEST.

"OF FIGHTING THE ONLY WAY I COULD: WITH UNMATCHED ELEGANCE AND CLASS.

"THE *HATERS* MAY NOT RESPECT ME.

DANCE COMPETITION

"BUT THEY ARE SURE AS *HELL* GOING TO ENVY ME."

33

WELL, YOU'VE CERTAINLY EARNED *MY* RESPECT.

SO TELL ME ABOUT THE DAY YOU GAINED YOUR POWERS.

WAS IT *TRAUMATIC?*

IN THE END, YES. BUT...

"...THE HOURS BEFORE THE *INCIDENT* WERE ACTUALLY QUITE LOVELY.

"THAT'S WHEN I MET ADAM."

YOU'RE INCREDIBLE!

THANKS.

THAT ACCENT. AMERICAN OR CANADIAN?

AMERICAN, AFTER A FASHION.

YOU LOT ARE A *MESS*, AREN'T YOU? ALTHOUGH I SUPPOSE WE'RE NOT DOING ANY BETTER.

HALF THE REASON I GOT OUT. BUT REALLY I'M ON A BIG GLOBE-TROTTING QUEST TO, I DUNNO, FIND MYSELF.

ANY LUCK?

WELL. I JUST STARTED LAST WEEK.

BUT I THINK MY PASSION IS *DANCE!* YOU KNOW, I'M GREAT AT THE WALTZ.

WE'LL SEE ABOUT THAT.

34

"WE SPENT THE NIGHT DANCING."

UH. YOU'RE LEADING?

OH, DEFINITELY.

THIS IS TERRIFYING.

AND THAT'S *WHY I'M* LEADING.

NOT BAD!

WOOH!

LET'S HAVE A DRINK.

ALMOST TIME.

SECURE THE EXITS AND WAIT FOR MY CALL.

"AND DRINKING."

CHEERS!

SO ARE YOU AND YOUR DANCE PARTNER, YOU KNOW...

MARTIN? *GOD*, NO. OUR RELATIONSHIP IS STRICTLY PROFESSIONAL.

NICE.

TWO-TIME CHAMPION IN BUENOS AIRES, AND I'M *STILL* NOT GOOD ENOUGH FOR MY PARENTS.

JESUS! THAT'S SO UNFAIR!

I LIKE HELPING PEOPLE, I GUESS. BUT I FELT LIKE I GOT KINDA...FORCED INTO MED SCHOOL BY MY FOLKS.

AND ONE DAY, I'M CRAMMING FOR MY EXAMS, AND I THINK TO MYSELF "WHY THE HELL AM I EVEN HERE?" COULDN'T THINK OF AN ANSWER, SO I WALKED.

THERE, THERE.

36

FORGET ABOUT ALL THAT MOROSE STUFF.

¡BAILAMOS!

YOU NEVER TOLD ME YOUR NAME.

ADAM LAND.

LAND? SERIOUSLY? THAT'S MY--

BLAM BLAM

EVERYONE GET ON YOUR KNEES!

I CAN'T BREATHE!

BLAM BLAM BLAM

BLAM

MARTIN!

DON'T FUCKING MOVE!

PLEASE, LET ME HELP HIM--

I SAW YOU DANCE EARLIER.

WITH THE MAN WE SHOT. RIGHT?

YOU'RE PERFORMERS?

WE CAN'T EXPECT A DECENT RANSOM FROM THE ENTERTAINMENT.

BLAM

38

WAIT! I'M *RICH!*

MY TRUST FUND IS BIGGER THAN TEXAS. DON'T HURT ANYONE. I'LL COOPERATE.

I WISH THAT WAS TRUE.

IT IS!

THEN WHY IS YOU IN AN EIGHTY-DOLLAR OFF-THE-RACK SUIT FROM JACEY'S MENSWEAR?

JUST MY LUCK WE'D GET THE ONE SARTORIALIST TERROR GROUP.

WELL, IT WAS WORTH A SHOT.

HEY.

IT WAS NICE MEETING YOU.

"AS I STARED DOWN THE BARREL OF THAT GUN, HOLDING ADAM'S HAND SO TIGHTLY...

"...A WARMTH SEEMED TO BLOOM BETWEEN OUR SKINS...

"...AND EXPLODE."

39

"LITERALLY.

"NOBODY ELSE SURVIVED--NOT THE TERRORISTS, NOT THE DANCERS. *JUST US.*

"WE'VE BEEN RUNNING EVER SINCE.

"UNABLE TO TOUCH. UNABLE TO ESCAPE EACH OTHER.

"UNABLE TO PREDICT WHAT WILL HAPPEN IF WE DO EITHER."

"WHAT *SPECIFICALLY* HAPPENS WHEN YOU TOUCH? HELP ME UNDERSTAND, ELAKSHI."

"I REALLY CAN'T."

"TRY. WHAT HAPPENS?"

"THE MANIFESTATION OF *NIGHTMARES.*"

40

WE'RE MAKING PROGRESS.

HOWEVER, I *REALLY* NEED TO SPEAK WITH ADAM.

YOUR POWERS ARE SO CLOSELY ENTWINED THAT YOUR TREATMENT NEEDS TO BE JOINED, TOO.

HE'S... BUSY TODAY.

101 METRES

WISH I COULD HELP YOU, BUDDY, BUT RULES ARE RULES.

NOPE.

YOU DON'T HAVE VISITING HOURS?

JUST FIVE MINUTES. I'M WORRIED. SHE WAS REALLY UPSET LAST NIGHT.

IT'S A PRIVACY MATTER.

IF YOU HAVE A PROBLEM WITH OUR RULES, TALK TO WIN.

I WILL.

THUNK

41

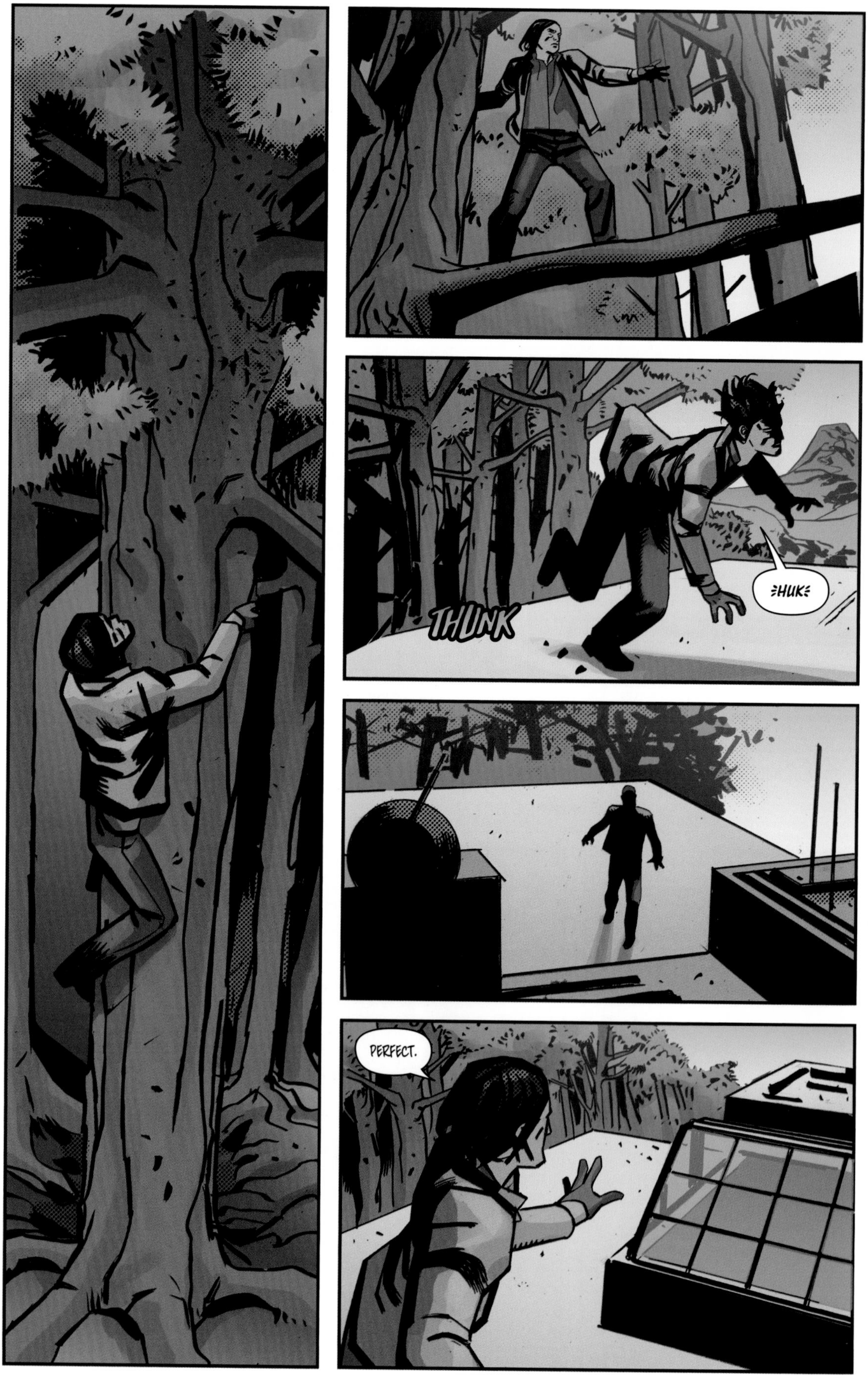
THUNK
HUK
PERFECT.

GOD! THESE PEOPLE HAVE THE WORST TASTE.

COAST LOOKS CLEAR, THOUGH.

C'MON.

KLIK

THIS IS THE SECOND TIME WE'VE COVERED THEIR SHIFT.

I'LL MAKE A REPORT DURING THE NEXT STAFF MEETING.

BEEP

GOD, NO.

44

I'M SO *HAPPY* YOU'RE HERE, MR. LAND.

Y'ALL HAVE UNTIL THE COUNT OF THREE TO BACK OFF.

THREE!

OOOF.

T.THOK

HANDS UP!

SURE THING, BOSS.

THUNK

HRGH!

TIE HIM UP, BOYS.

I DON'T WANT TO DO *EVERYTHING* AROUND HERE.

IT'S A SHAME ADAM IS SO RESISTANT TO TREATMENT.

I CAN DO IT WITHOUT HIM, THOUGH, RIGHT?

YES.

BUT WE MIGHT NEED TO TAKE A *DIFFERENT* APPROACH.

I'LL SEE YOU AGAIN TONIGHT, ELAKSHI.

BE WELL.

WHAT IS IT?

THAT NEW GUY. ADAM.

I THINK HE'S GONNA CAUSE TROUBLE.

ADAM HAS BEEN HANDLED.

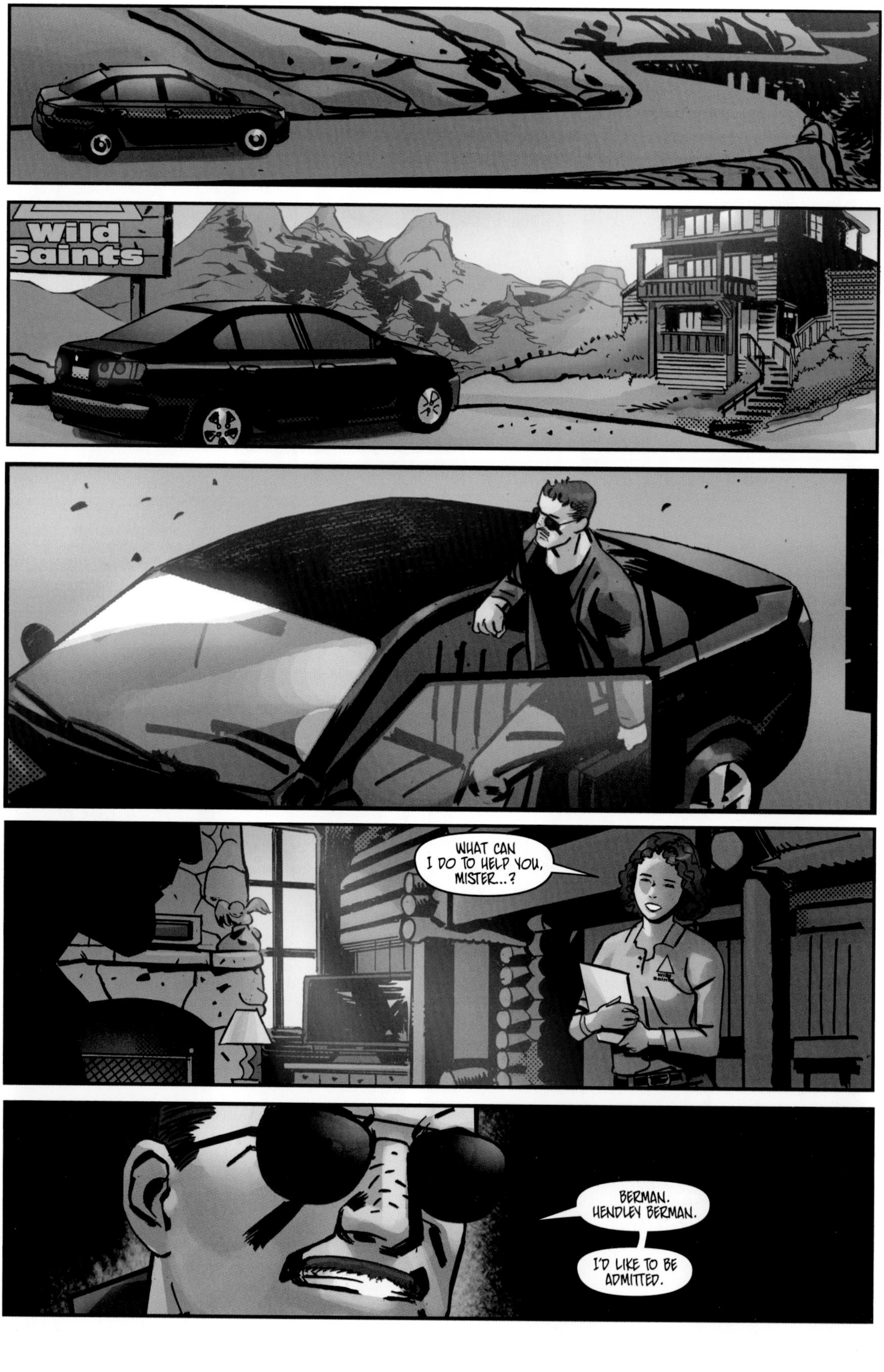
Wild Saints
WHAT CAN I DO TO HELP YOU, MISTER...?
BERMAN. HENDLEY BERMAN.
I'D LIKE TO BE ADMITTED.

COLORADO
WILD SAINTS LODGE

WHEN DID YOU FIRST UNDERSTAND YOUR POWERS, HENDLEY?

IT HAPPENED ON A CROWDED STREET.

A MAN SLIPPED HIS HAND INTO MY JACKET POCKET. TRIED TO STEAL MY WALLET.

"I INCAPACITATED HIM WITH ONE BLOW."

"SHATTERED HIS NOSE. IT WAS DISGUSTING."

HOW DID THAT MAKE YOU FEEL?

"LIKE *MY* NOSE WAS BROKEN.

"OH. YOU MEAN *EMOTIONALLY*."

"YES, MR. HENDLEY, EMOTIONALLY."

"ANNOYED. HE GOT AWAY.

51

"BUT, I GUESS ... THAT'S WHEN I TRULY APPRECIATED THE PRICE OF MY INVULNERABILITY. DOES THAT MAKE SENSE?

CRASH

"I FEEL EVERY BROKEN BONE.

BANG

"EVERY BULLET HOLE."

EVERY SINGLE ONE. EVERY DAY IS PAINFUL, IN MY LINE OF WORK. THAT'S WHY I'M HERE.

52

PICK UP THE *PHONE*, ADAM.

201 METRES

HEY! WHAT HAS TWO THUMBS AND IS BUSY RIGHT NOW?

THIS GUY! LEAVE A MESSAGE AFTER THE TONE.

WHERE *ARE* YOU AND YOUR TWO THUMBS?!

UM. LISTEN. I KNOW I SAY THIS ABOUT EVERY MUSCLEY STRANGER, BUT...

...THERE WAS A BIG MAN AT GROUP THERAPY, AND I THINK IT'S *HIM*.

AM I JUST PARANOID? GOD. I DON'T KNOW. *PLEASE* CALL ME BACK.

ELAKSHI! KITTYHAWK! SOMEBODY!

IT'S JUST YOU AND ME, I'M AFRAID. EVERYONE ELSE IS HAVING LUNCH IN TOWN.

DON'T BE SO *DRAMATIC*, ADAM. I'M HERE TO HELP.

SORRY TO KEEP YOU WAITING. MY GROUP THERAPY SESSION RAN LATE.

WE HAVE THE MOST FASCINATING NEW PATIENT.

YOU MEAN *VICTIM?*

OUR METHODS ARE EXTREME, BUT THEY WORK. LET ME HELP YOU.

NO?

PLEASE. DO IT FOR ELAKSHI. WITHOUT YOUR COOPERATION, SHE'LL BE MISERABLE FOREVER.

AS YOU KNOW, YOUR POWERS ARE LINKED.

SHE ENTRUSTED ME WITH HER PAINFUL MEMORIES. HER PSYCHIC TRAUMA.

WE WERE ON THE CUSP OF A BREAKTHROUGH. NOW, IT'S YOUR TURN.

WHAT ARE YOU, MY SIXTH GRADE GUIDANCE COUNSELOR?

USE OF HUMOR AS A DEFLECTION TACTIC. PREDICTABLE.

IN THAT CASE, WE'LL NEED A DIFFERENT APPROACH.

PHYSICAL TRAUMA SHOULD DO THE TRICK. IT USUALLY DOES, WHEN I CAN'T WORK WITH *EMOTIONAL* SINCERITY.

ON SECOND THOUGHT, LET ME TELL YOU ABOUT MY HORRIBLE CHILDHOOD.

"I BARELY ATE.

"MY DAD WAS NEVER AROUND. AND WHEN HE WAS, HE'D HIT ME.

54

"THINGS WENT DOWNHILL AFTER PUBERTY.

"I WAS MISERABLE AND ISOLATED, AND MY MOM WOULD WORK ME TO DEATH."

ADAM, ADAM, ADAM... LYING ONLY PUTS OFF THE HEALING PROCESS.

WHAT CAN I SAY, MAN? LIFE WAS GOOD!

YOU'VE NEVER EXPERIENCED *ANY* MISERY OR GRIEF? NEVER LOST SOMEBODY YOU LOVE?

I'M NOT TELLING A PIECE OF SHIT LIKE YOU ABOUT MY SWEET GRANDMAMA, GOD REST HER SOUL.

HARD WAY IT IS.

53 METRES

EXCUSE ME!

55

MISTER HENDLEY, RIGHT?

UH. YOU CAN LET GO NOW.

WE NEED TO CHAT.

WHAT? NO! LET ME GO!

I'M SERIOUS!

OOF!

56

28 METRES

15 METRES

TK-TK

THERE YOU ARE!

WIN IS WAITING FOR YOU.

WHAT'S BEHIND THIS DOOR?

OH, *THAT* DOOR?

I *THINK* IT LEADS TO THE BOILER ROOM.

COME ON!

ELAKSHI! PLEASE HAVE A SEAT.

YOU'RE UPSET.

WHY?

WHY ELSE? ADAM. I CAN'T FIND HIM ANYWHERE.

AH! EVERYBODY EXCEPT ELISE AND ME ARE VISITING TOWN. A SPONTANEOUS TRIP.

ADAM WAS MORE THAN HAPPY FOR THE CHANGE OF SCENERY. YOU CAN JOIN HIM LATER.

HOW FAR AWAY IS THE NEAREST TOWN?

WE CAN *WASTE* YOUR SESSION TALKING ABOUT ADAM...

...OR WE CAN MAKE ACTUAL PROGRESS.

LET'S DISCUSS TRAUMA.

I'VE ALREADY *TOLD* YOU EVERYTHING.

I WAS AFRAID OF THAT. NO WORRIES.

LIKE I SAID. WHEN *EMOTIONAL* PAIN ISN'T THE KEY...

...CORPOREAL *THERAPY* MAY HELP.

WHAT THE--?!

59

DON'T BE AFRAID. THE PAIN WILL FREE YOU.

TRUST ME.

OH, HELL NO.

HELP! SOMEBODY!

WEREN'T YOU LISTENING? NOBODY CAN HEAR YOU.

GET OFF ME!

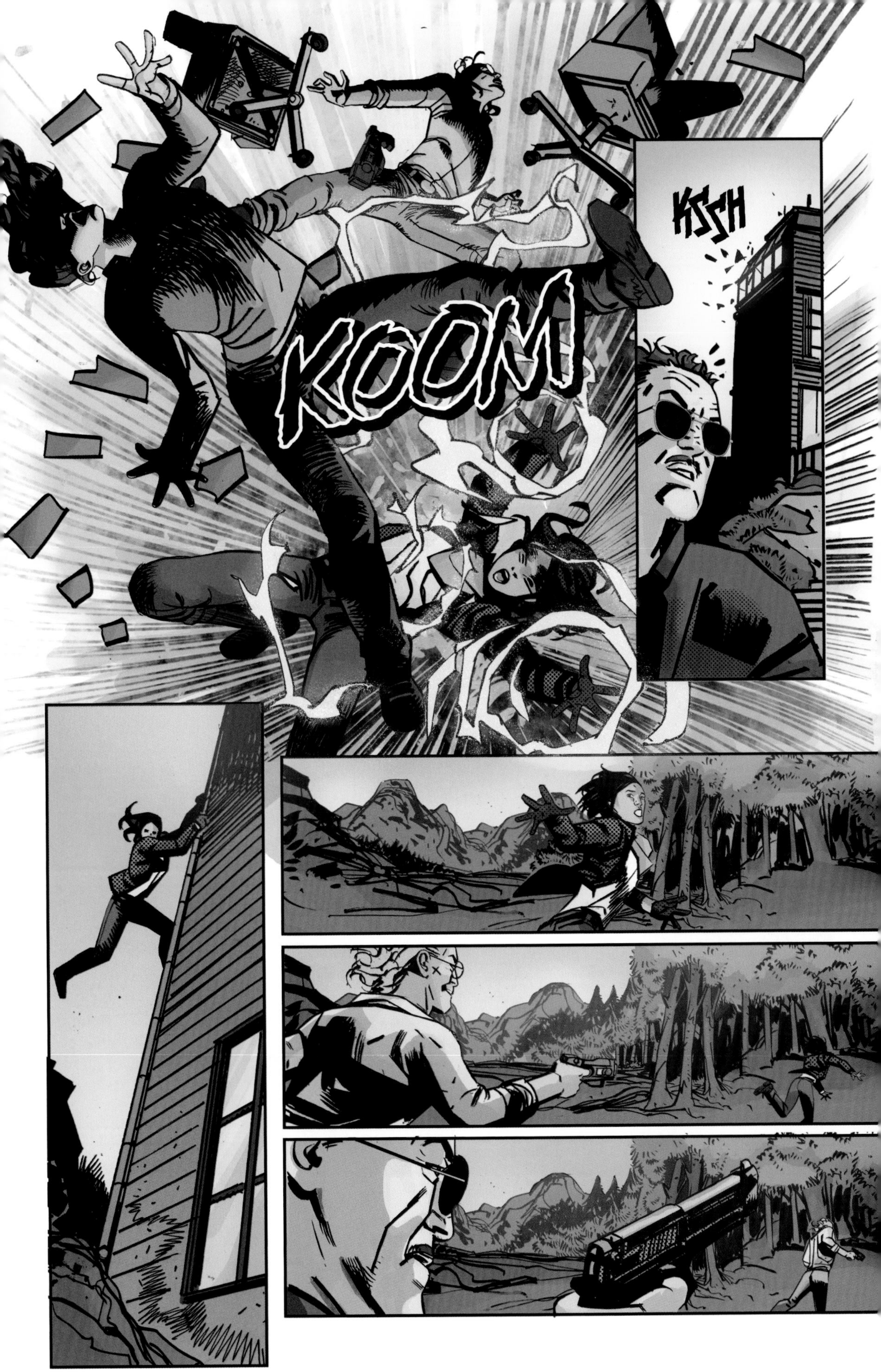
KOOM
KSSH

YOU WERE DOING *SO WELL,* ELAKSHI!

WANKER!

398 METRES

NO, NO, NO!

WE'RE GETTING TOO FAR APART.

684 METRES

CRNCH CRNCH

HYAAAA!

CRK

Y--YOU! WHAT DO YOU WANT?

WHERE'S YOUR PARTNER?

63

I *KNEW* YOU LOOKED FAMILIAR.

YOU'RE THE MAN WHO'S BEEN CHASING US FOR MONTHS.

THAILAND, NEW ZEALAND, CHINA, BRAZIL, AND NOW BLOODY COLORADO!

I'M SO *SICK* OF RUNNING!

I WILL NOT ASK AGAIN. WHERE IS ADAM LAND?

I DON'T BLOODY KNOW! WHAT AM I, HIS NANNY?

MAYBE I CAN HELP.

HENDLEY BERMAN. WITH A GUN. DARE I ASK?

IF YOU HURT ADAM, I'LL...

BE FREE?

IN MY PROFESSIONAL OPINION, THAT'S THE *CURE*. HIS DEATH WILL BREAK THE CURSE THAT BINDS YOU. ONCE AND FOR ALL.

ISN'T THAT WHAT YOU WANT? WHO *IS* THIS MAN TO YOU, ANYWAY? JUST SOME STRANGER YOU GOT STUCK WITH.

YOUR FREEDOM IS *SO CLOSE*.

64

ENOUGH OF THIS.

BANG BANG

SON OF A...!

YOU WANTED TO KNOW MY TRAUMA, FLETCHER?

I'LL DEMONSTRATE WHAT HAPPENS WHEN ADAM AND I GET TOO FAR APART.

1075 METRES

"BRACE YOURSELVES, GENTLEMEN. THINGS ARE ABOUT TO GET *WILD*."

HRRRGH. C'MON.

I'LL SHOW YOU WHY OUR POWERS GIVE ME NIGHTMARES.

1078 METRES WARNING!

65

SCRRREEEEEE

EASY. JUST A LITTLE TO THE RIGHT.

OW. OWOWOW.

LIKE HARRY FREAKING HOUDINI!

GONNA SET UP A NICE SURPRISE FOR YOU, MR. WINSOME.

66

UH. HEY THERE.

EL! WHAT ARE YOU DOING?

BEEP! BEEP! BEEP!

3540 METRES

PLEASE NO. ELAKSHI!

SOMEBODY LET ME OUT OF HERE! BEFORE...

THNK THNK

NNNNNG! IT'S TOO LATE.

ELAKSHI...

"...I'M SO SORRY."

BANG BANG

STOP! NOT ANOTHER STEP!

WHAT CHOICE DO I HAVE?

YOU'LL NEVER LEAVE US ALONE.

WAIT! YOU--

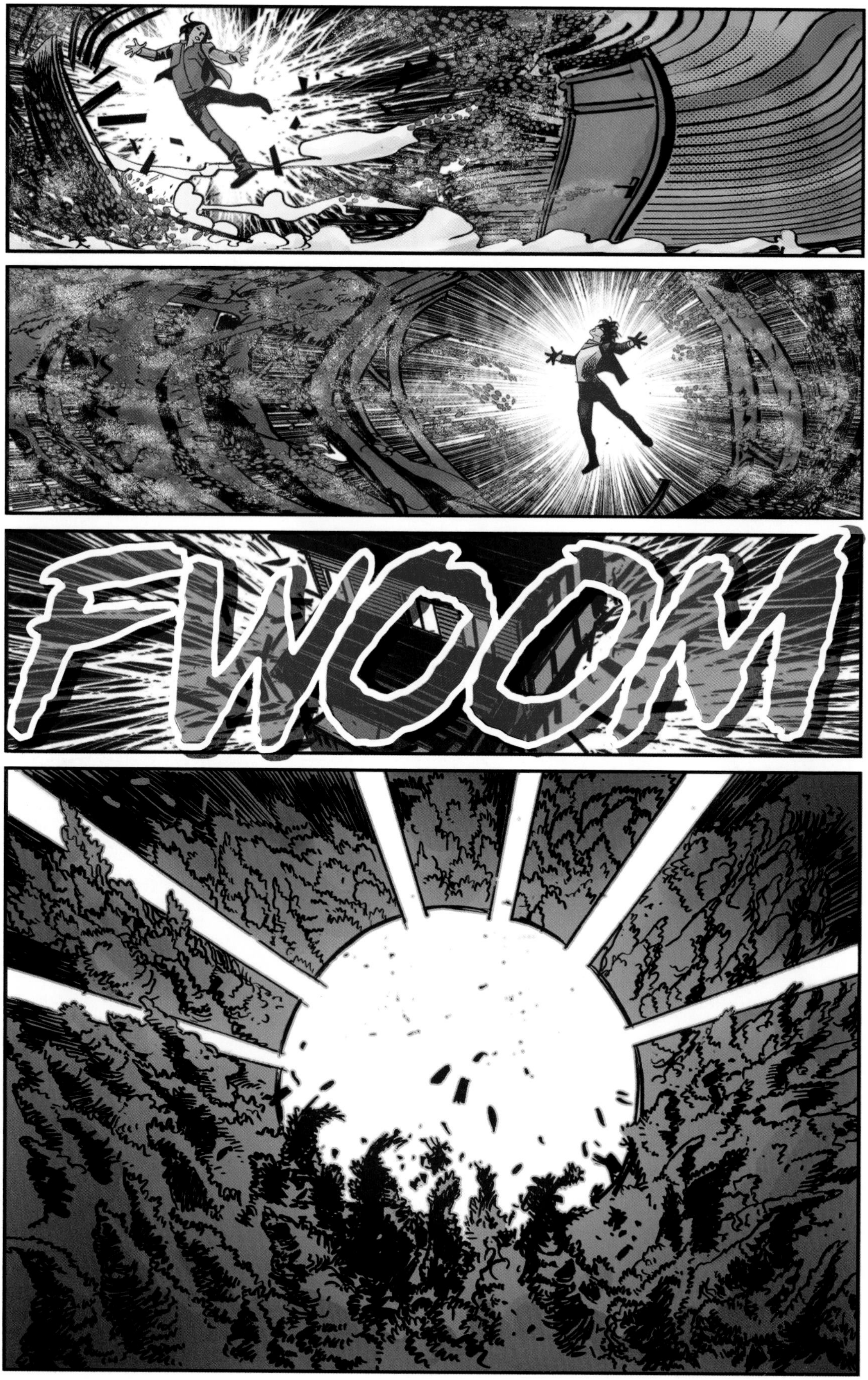
FWOOM

4

COLORADO
LOCATION: UNKNOWN

IT'S COMING SOON. TRUST ME.

TELL ME, SIMON. WERE YOU THERE IN '68?

IT WAS SUPPOSED TO BE A *REVOLUTION.* WE WERE SO SURE WE WERE GOING TO CHANGE THE WORLD.

REMAKE IT IN OUR IMAGE.

TAKE IT BY THE THROAT.

CHANGE THE WORLD? NICE PLATITUDE...

...BUT WE DON'T GET TO PICK AND CHOOSE THE REALITY WE LIVE IN.

85 metres

"PERHAPS *YOU* DON'T, SIMON."

"BUT LIMITS ARE FOR THE *WEAK*."

AND IF THERE'S ONE THING I'M NOT...

50 metres

...IT'S WEAK.

NOBODY WOULD ACCUSE YOU OF THAT, SYLVIA.

SO WHAT DID YOU HAVE IN MIND?

AH AH AH.

SLOWLY.

WE BUILD SLOWLY.

"YOU MAKE THEM FEAR YOU.

"YOU MAKE THEM NEED YOU."

SO ALL YOU NEED TO DO RIGHT NOW IS DECIDE.

DO YOU WANT A PLACE IN MY NEW WORLD OR NOT?

0 metres

75

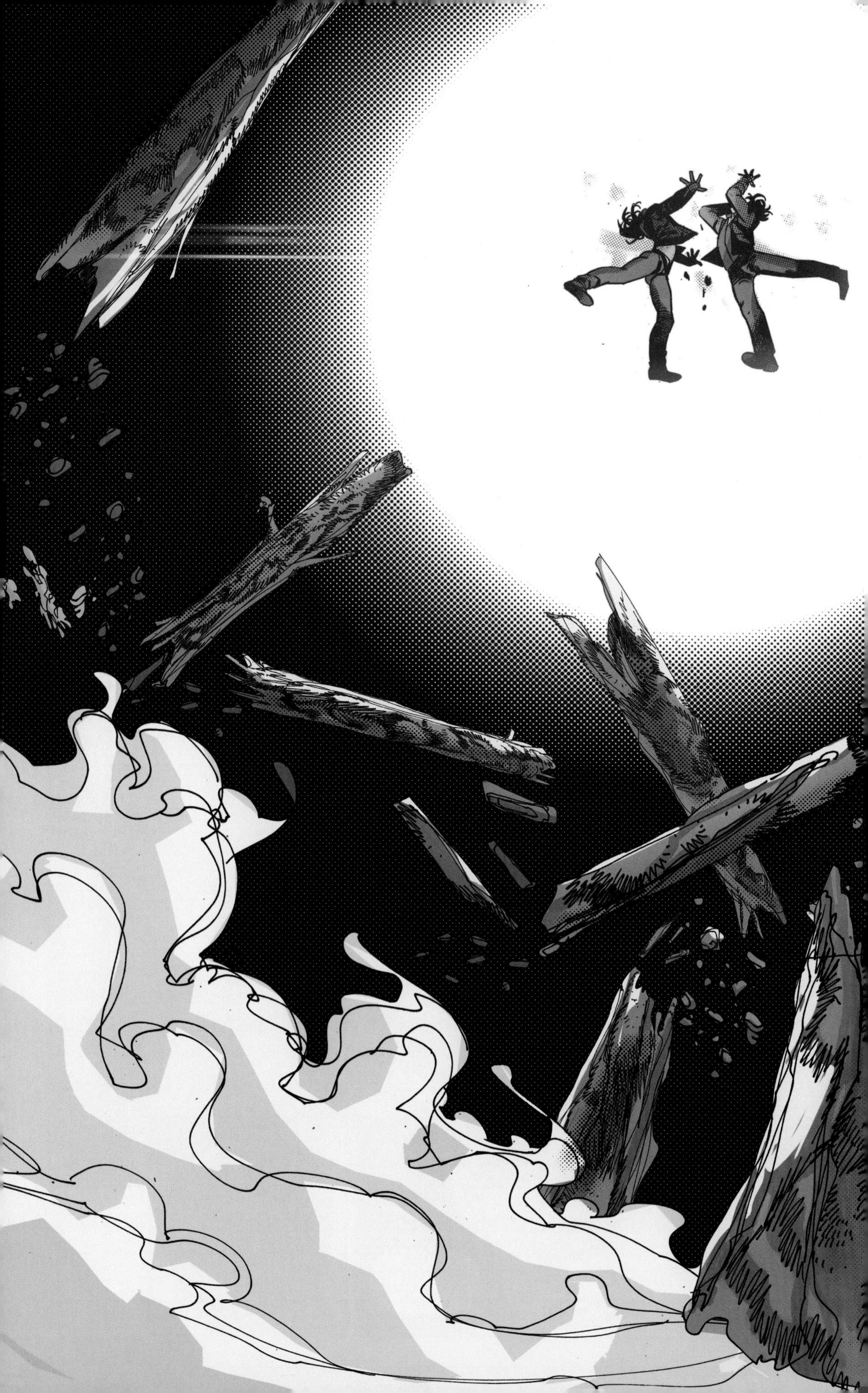

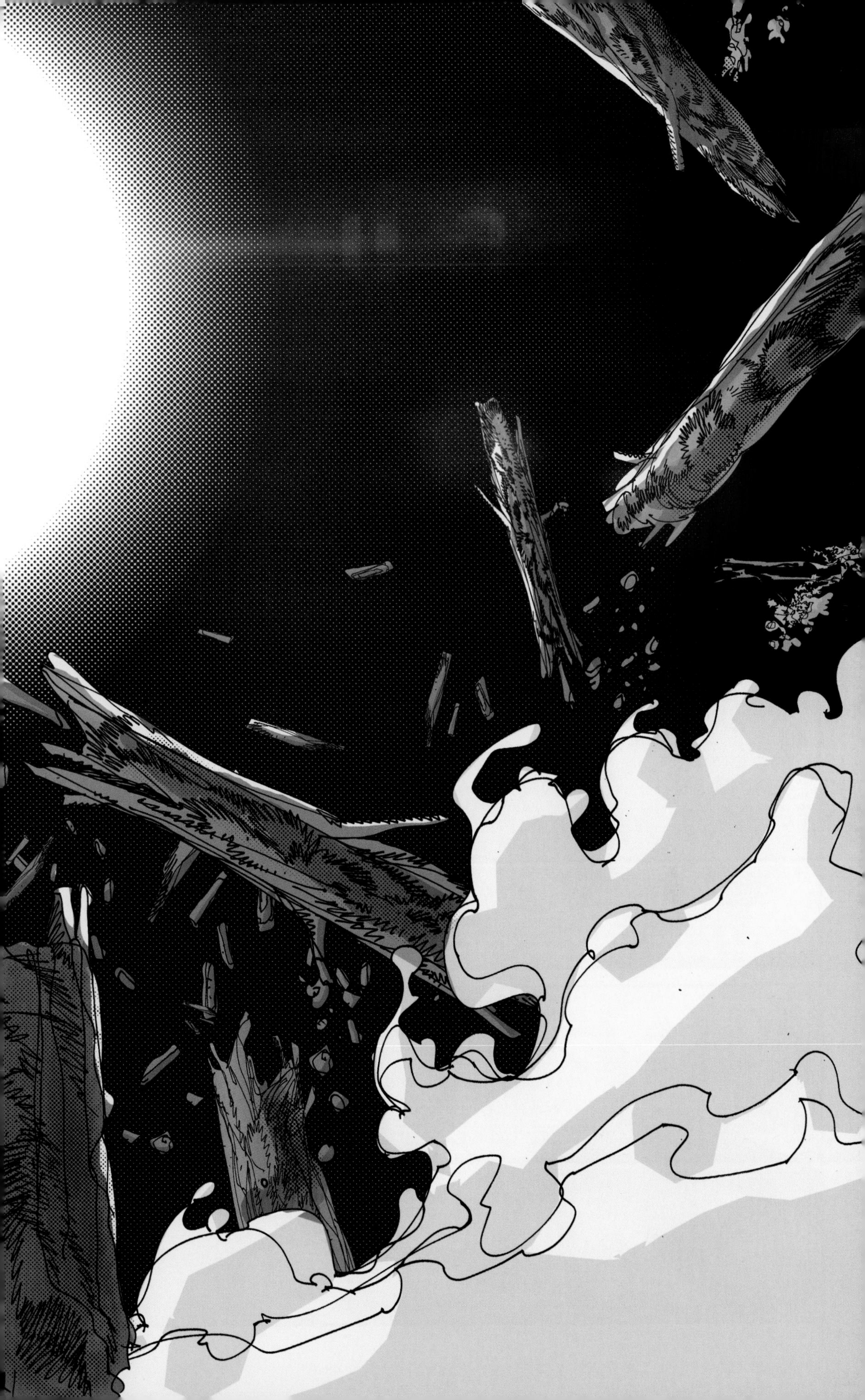

WHUMP

WHAM

EL... ARE YOU OKAY?

...YEAH =KOFF= I'M FINE.

CONSIDERING WHAT JUST HAPPENED...

...I'M GLAD *SOMEONE* IS.

THANK GOD WE'RE FORTY MILES FROM THE NEAREST GAS STATION.

EL--

NOT NOW. WE NEED TO GO.

AND *FAST*.

WHAT DO--

WIN IS AFTER US-- AND SO IS OUR *MYSTERY MAN*.

MYSTERY MAN?

MYSTERY MAN, ADAM! DO I NEED TO SPELL IT OUT?

HE FOLLOWED US HERE. HE WAS IN GROUP SESSIONS. HE *JUST* TRIED TO KILL ME.

YOU DON'T GET IT, ADAM...

THAT MEANS HE WAS IN THE BLAST RADIUS, RIGHT? PROBLEM SOLVED. *FINALLY!*

"HE CAN'T BE KILLED."

HENDLEY, WAS IT?

HENDLEY BERMAN. THAT'S AN ALIAS, ISN'T IT?

SHOULD HAVE KNOWN. MINE IS, TOO. THE BEST ONES *ALWAYS* ARE.

YOUR FAKE AMERICAN ACCENT IS *TERRIBLE*, HOWEVER.

YOU A BOUNTY HUNTER? ASSASSIN? NOT THAT IT MATTERS, I SUPPOSE.

NOT LONG AGO, I LEARNED THAT OTHER PEOPLE'S SUFFERING *FED* ME. GAVE ME POWER. GAVE ME *LIFE*.

THAT'S WHY I'LL BE THE ONLY SURVIVOR OF THIS TRAGIC EXPLOSION.

WAIT...NOTHING'S HAPPENING.

WHY IS NOTHING HAPPENING?

80

=URK=

WEREN'T YOU LISTENING DURING THERAPY, VAMPIRE?

I'M NOT ONE OF YOUR LITTLE VICTIMS.

LET GO OF ME... LET ME~

I CAN SEE IT...I CAN SEE MY PAIN IN YOUR EYES...

...AREN'T YOU FINDING IT A LITTLE HARD...TO BREATHE?

GAH!

=KOFF KOFF=

I LISTENED WELL ENOUGH TO KNOW...

...YOU NEED THIS.

YOU ALSO NEED A THERAPIST, HENDLEY! A REAL ONE. HAH!

81

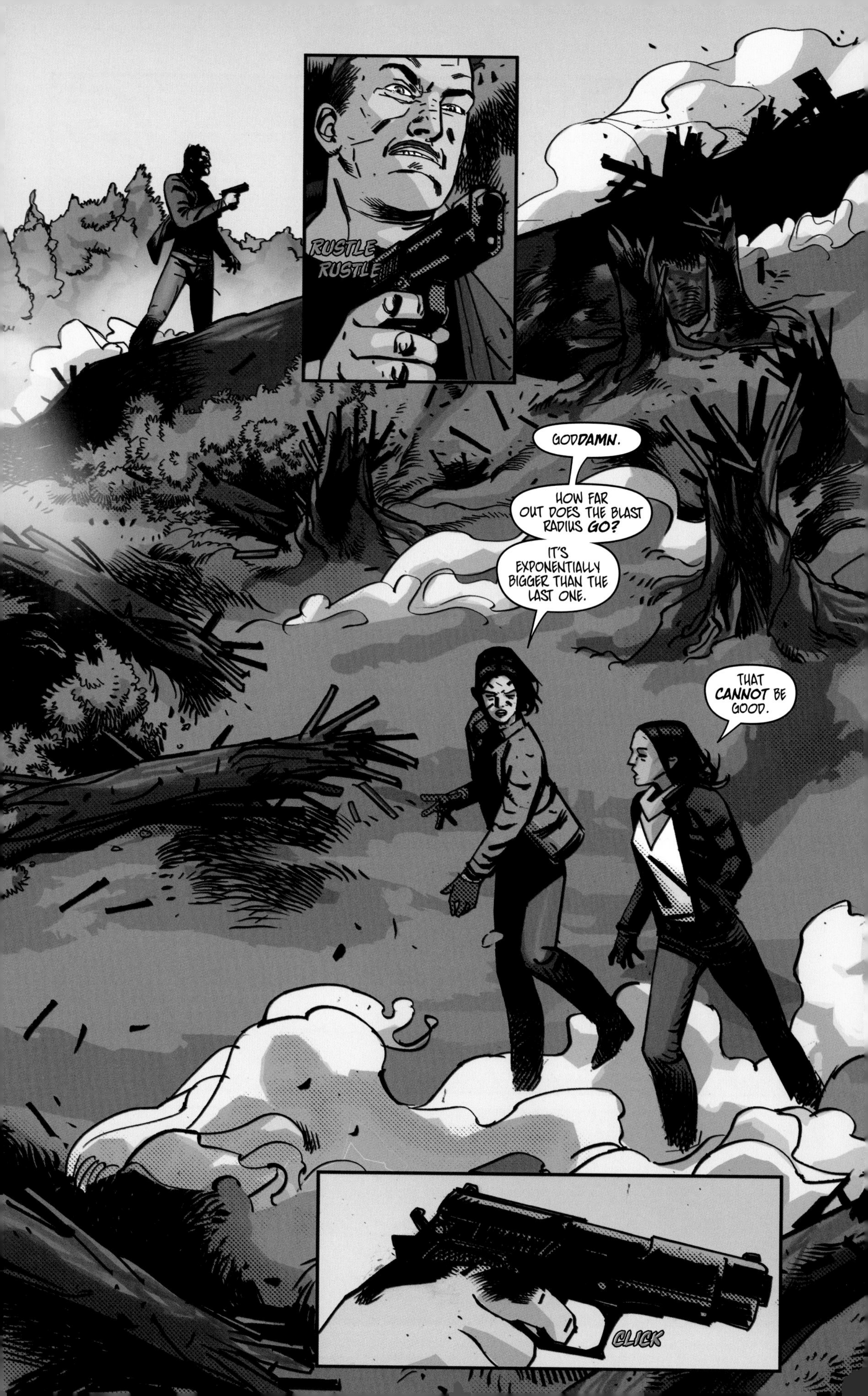
RUSTLE RUSTLE
GODDAMN.
HOW FAR OUT DOES THE BLAST RADIUS GO?
IT'S EXPONENTIALLY BIGGER THAN THE LAST ONE.
THAT CANNOT BE GOOD.
CLICK

BLAM BLAM BLAM

SHIT!

ADAM! GET DOWN!

BLAM BLAM BLAM

ANY IDEAS?

WE COULD AWKWARDLY FLEE BACKWARDS WHILE I HOLD UP A DUBIOUSLY RELIABLE REPELLING FIELD AND HE SLOWLY STALKS US TO DEATH. SO. NO.

NO IDEAS.

HOW MANY BULLETS ARE THERE IN A MAGAZINE? HE SHOULD BE RUNNIN' OUT OF AMMO...

CLICK

...OR NOT!

BLAM

STOP!

PLEASE, STOP!

83

OKAY. I'M GONNA TRY AND TAKE HIS GUN.

WORKED LAST TIME.

HEY, MUSCLES!

UNNNG...

THUMP

84

WHY...? WHY ARE YOU DOING THIS?

YOU'RE A WALKING TUNGUSKA, YOU REALIZE THAT?

LOOK AT EVERYTHING YOU'VE DONE.

BRITISH INTELLIGENCE SENT ME.

AH!

THE LEGENDARY MI6.

I KNOW WHAT I'VE DONE.

WE'RE TRYING TO FIND A CURE!

WE CAN'T RISK YOU FAILING.

≣HUP≣

YOU'LL HAVE TO TELL THE QUEEN I'M NOT GOING BACK UNTIL WE FIGURE THIS OUT!

WILD SAINTS
...OR WHAT'S LEFT OF IT

JUST BE GRATEFUL THAT YOU WEREN'T HERE WHEN IT HAPPENED.

WHAT ABOUT MY FRIEND?

SHE'S STILL MISSING. MAYBE--

STOP *FIXATING*. FOCUS ON THE POSITIVES.

IT'S A GOOD THING WIN SENT EVERYONE INTO TOWN THIS MORNING.

EVERYONE EXCEPT FOR YOU, WIN, AND THOSE NEWBIES. BIT STRANGE, NO?

MAYBE YOU SHOULD WAIT WITH THE OTHER PATIENTS--

HELP ME. PLEASE, GOD, HELP ME.

WIN? WE THOUGHT YOU WERE--

RUMORS OF MY DEATH, ET CETERA.

WERE THERE ANY CASUALTIES?

I'VE FELT BETTER.

Wild Saints

...OH, ELISE. YOUR ARM.

I'M SO SORRY.

86

HEY--!

I'M SO, SO SORRY.

WHAT ARE YOU DOING? LET ME GO!

WE HAD A DEAL--!

YOU WILL FIND IT DIFFICULT TO ENFORCE A CONTRACT WITH SOMEONE WHO DOESN'T EXIST.

AAAGH!

THANK YOU, ELISE. I FEEL BETTER ALREADY.

WITH YOUR GENEROUS SACRIFICE, I'LL BE ABLE TO ESCAPE.

THEN, IT'S JUST A MATTER OF FINDING ANOTHER NEW NAME.

YOU HUMAN PIECE OF TRASH!

THOK

≡UNF≡

ELISE... DON'T LEAVE ME...

I'LL DIE!

GOOD.

87

DON'T EVEN THINK ABOUT IT.

I CAN USE MY POWER TO REPEL YOU AS MANY TIMES AS IT TAKES.

LIKE YOU'RE AN ANGRY HUMAN PINBALL!

YOU WANNA KEEP THROWING ME INTO TREES? GO AHEAD.

I'M *INVULNERABLE.* ALL I GOTTA DO IS OUTLAST YOU.

THE GUN, ADAM!

HRGH!

THANKS, BRO!

I ALREADY *SAID* YOU CAN'T HURT ME. WHAT DO YOU THINK YOU'RE GONNA DO WITH THAT GUN?

DUMP THE AMMO.

WE'RE NOT GOING TO DO *ANYTHING* WITH YOUR GUN.

AND NOW, NEITHER ARE YOU.

K'CHAK

88

I WAS THERE AT YOUR GROUP SESSION, MR. MIG.

AND I KNOW THE PRICE OF YOUR INVULNERABILITY.

CUTE. YOU THINK I NEED A *GUN* TO KILL YOU?

SURE, YOU COULD *TRY* TO KILL US WITH YOUR BARE HANDS. BUT YOU'D FEEL EVERY BLOW.

EVERY BRUISE, EVERY BROKEN BONE, EVERY CUT, SCRAPE, SCAR, OR GASH.

MAYBE YOU'D WIN. OR MAYBE YOU'D JUST SEND YOUR OWN SYSTEM INTO SHOCK AS YOU TORTURED YOURSELF WITH YOUR VICTIMS' PAIN.

CHOOSE FAST. WON'T BE LONG TILL FEDS SWARM THIS PLACE.

THINK THEY'LL APPRECIATE MIG ON THEIR TURF?

WHAT'S THAT? DO I HEAR A HELICOPTER ALREADY?

SO WHAT'LL IT BE?

YOU THAT MUCH OF A SUPERMAN THAT YOU CAN HANDLE THAT KIND OF PAIN?

YOU SMUG LITTLE...

THNK

THIS TIME.

NEW MEXICO
DAYS LATER

IT'S SUPPOSED TO BE RIGHT AROUND HERE.

SO. WE'RE OKAY WITH THIS, THEN?

HM? WHAT? THE SUNGLASSES? THEY LOOK GREAT!

NO. KITTYHAWK. WE DON'T HAVE *ANY IDEA* WHO SHE IS OR WHY SHE'S LOOKING OUT FOR US.

BUT YET AGAIN, WE'RE TRUSTING HER TO SEND US TO SAFETY. HOW'D THAT WORK OUT LAST TIME?

OH, *DISASTROUSLY*, BUT WE DON'T EXACTLY HAVE A BETTER OPTION.

WAIT. I THINK I SEE SOMETHING OFF THE ROAD.

THINK IT'S HER?

HO THERE!

YOU'LL FIND PASSPORTS AND A COUPLE OF PRE-PAID CARDS IN THERE, PLUS A SMALL SUPPLY OF CASH.

HAR HAR.

AND A GUN.

TRUST ME, YOU'LL NEED IT. CONSIDERING WHERE YOU'RE GOING.

DO WE GET TO KNOW WHERE THAT IS?

NOT NOW.

"YOU NEVER KNOW WHO MIGHT BE LISTENING."

STRANGELANDS
UNDERCOVER

Initial sketch for Elakshi and Adam by Yanick Paquette. This was one of the first final designs created for the H1 Ignition shared universe. Yanick included a suitcase to convey the fact that they were constantly traveling.

Original cover for **Strangelands #3** by Yanick Paquette. Colors by Bryan Valenza.

Original variant cover for **Strangelands #1** by Vanesa Del Rey. Colors by Lee Loughridge.

Original cover for **Strangelands** #4 by Yanick Paquette. Colors by Bryan Valenza.